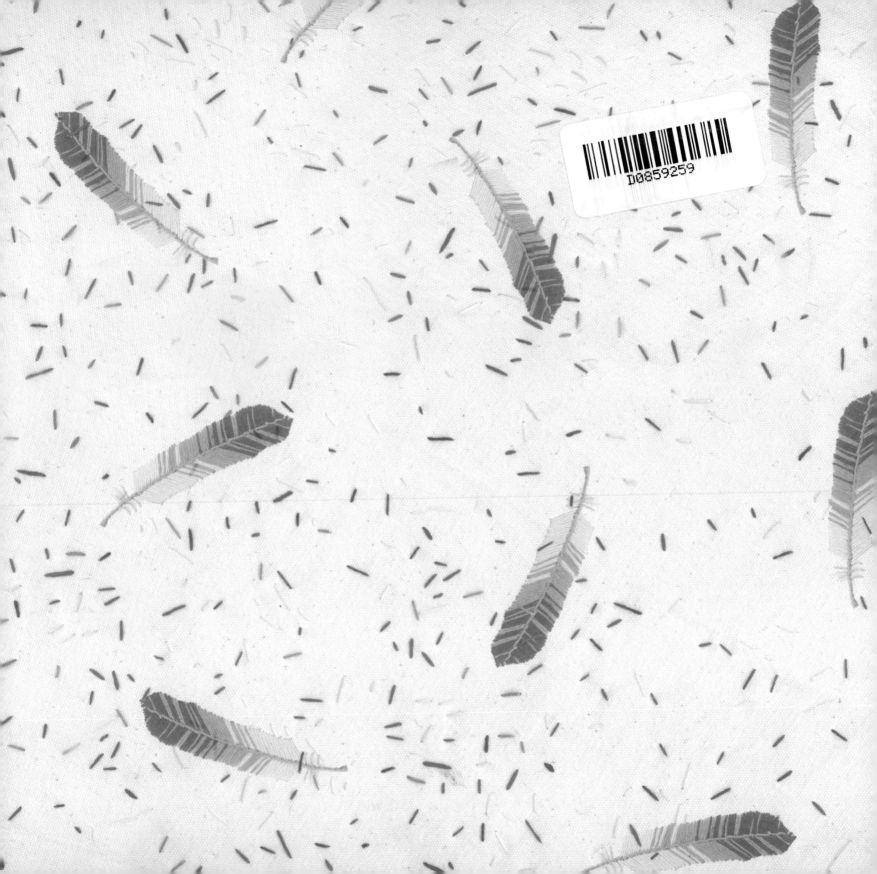

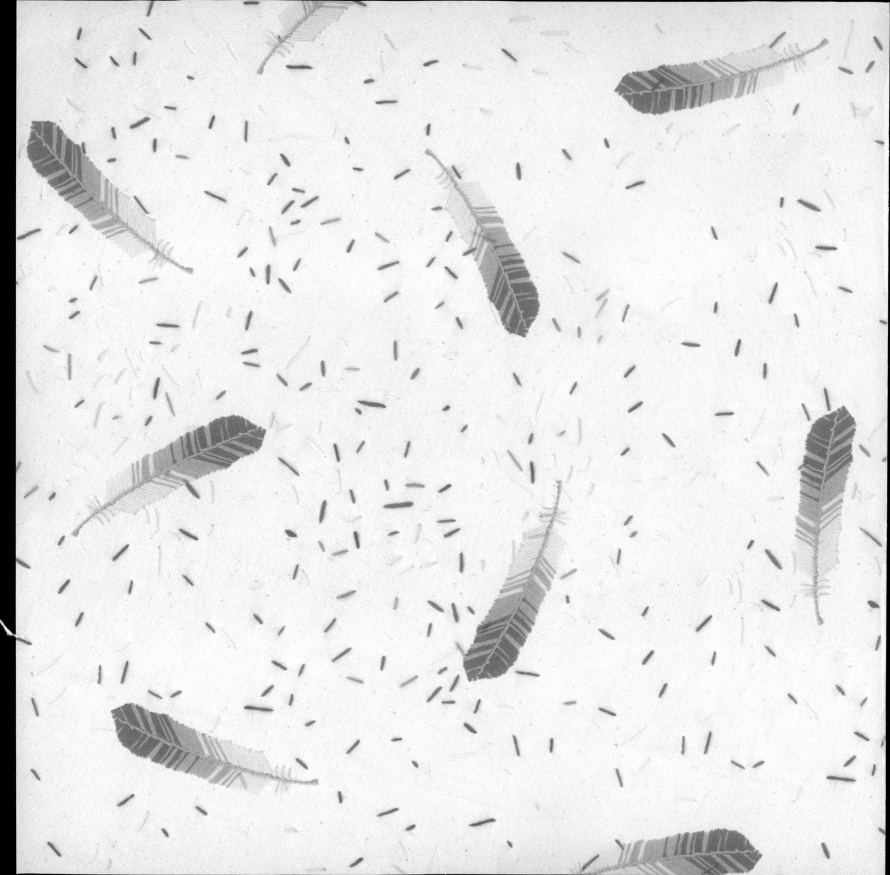

The Magical Rooster

Copyright © 2016 by Shanghai Press and Publishing Development Company, Ltd.

This book is edited and designed by the Editorial Committee of *Cultural China* series

Story and Illustrations: Li Jian
Translation: Yijin Wert

Editors: Wu Yuezhou, Anna Nguyen
Editorial Director: Zhang Yicong

Senior Consultants: Sun Yong, Wu Ying, Yang Xinci
Managing Director and Publisher: Wang Youbu

ISBN: 978-1-60220-995-4

Address any comments about *The Magical Rooster* to:

Better Link Press
99 Park Ave
New York, NY 10016
USA

or

Shanghai Press and Publishing Development Company, Ltd.
F 7 Donghu Road, Shanghai, China (200031)
Email: comments_betterlinkpress@hotmail.com

Printed in China by Shenzhen Donnelley Printing Co., Ltd.

1   3   5   7   9   10   8   6   4   2

花公鸡
The Magical Rooster

A Tale in English and Chinese

by Li Jian

Translated by Yijin Wert

Better Link Press

A long time ago, Tang Yun and his mother lived in a small village in the mountain. Yun's mother made beautiful and colorful hand embroideries with her capable hands.

很久以前，唐云和母亲生活在一个小山村里。他的母亲有一双灵巧的手，刺绣栩栩如生，非常精美。

Yun's mother made her living by selling the beautiful hand embroidered pieces. She worked very hard to support Yun with his schooling. Soon Yun reached the age when he could take the imperial exam in the Capital City.

唐云的母亲辛辛苦苦地绣着各种东西，卖了之后，将换得的钱供唐云读书。如今，唐云到了能去京城考试的年纪。

She could not sleep or eat knowing that her son had to travel thousands of miles by himself to take the test.

想到儿子要孤身一人、千里迢迢地去考试，母亲就睡不着觉，吃不下饭。

One day, Yun's mother realized that she had to do something for her son. She picked up her needles and thread and started to hand embroider Yun's outfit day and night.

有一天，母亲想到她该为儿子做些什么，于是拿起针线，没日没夜地为唐云绣起衣服来。

When it was time for Yun to go, his mother brought him the outfit with a rooster embroidered on it. She insisted that he should not take it off during his journey.

Yun started his long journey after saying good-bye to his mother.

唐云该出发了，母亲拿出一件绣着花公鸡的衣服让他穿在身上，嘱咐他路上千万不要脱下来。

唐云拜别母亲就启程了。

The road to the Capital City was far and long.

Yun travelled for three days without a break. Once Yun reached a large river, he had to stay for a night since the ferry would not leave until the next morning.

去京城的路又远又长。

唐云一口气走了三天，一条大河拦住了他的路。第二天早上才有渡船，唐云只好住在旅店里。

Early in the morning, the ferry was about to leave, but Yun laid in bed sound asleep tired from his travels. Suddenly, the embroidered rooster from his clothes jumped out to crow "cock-a-doodle-doo". Yun immediately woke up and caught the ferry in time.

又累又乏的唐云一直睡到大天亮还没有醒。渡船马上就要开走了。这时，母亲绣的花公鸡突然"喔喔"叫着，从衣服上跳出来，叫醒了唐云。

Yun still had ways to go on the road to the Capital City.

He stopped after traveling another three days. By this point, he was worried and tired, since he would miss the examination date if he didn't make it to the Capital City on time.

去京城的路又远又长。

唐云一口气又走了三天。如果不能按时到达京城，就会错过考试的日期，他又累又急。

Just then, Yun saw the magical rooster jump out of his outfit and crow a bold "cock-a-doodle-doo". The rooster began to grow bigger and bigger until it's large enough for Yun to ride on, which helped him continue the journey.

这时，母亲绣的花公鸡突然"喔喔"叫着，从衣服上跳出来，越变越大，直到可以驮起唐云快快赶路。

The road to the Capital City still felt far and long.

Within moments, a gust of cold wind blew in and it started to snow. Yun was shivering under his thin layer of clothes.

去京城的路又远又长。

一阵寒风吹过，天上突然飘起了雪花。衣服单薄的唐云冻得直发抖。

Sensing Yun felt very cold, the magical rooster crowed again "cock-a-doodle-doo". Then he covered Yun with his warm feathers. There Yun was able to have a good night's sleep.

神奇的花公鸡发现唐云瑟瑟发抖，便"喔喔"叫起来，让他钻进温暖的羽毛里，暖暖地睡了一觉。

The road to the Capital City was far and long, but Tang Yun had a companion.

In a forest, a greedy fox began to hunt the rooster. The magical rooster started to crow "cock-a-doodle-doo" and shook with fear.

去京城的路又远又长，但是唐云有了一个小伙伴。

他们来到一座森林，一只馋嘴的狐狸要抓花公鸡。花公鸡"咕咕"叫着，害怕得直发抖。

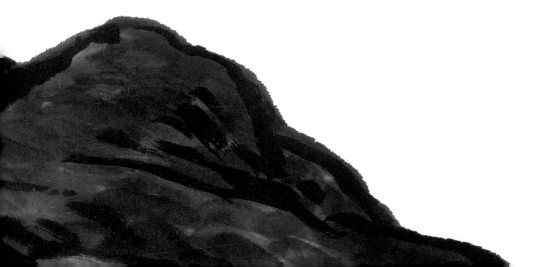

The rooster has been such a great helper to Yun. He was determined to save the kind rooster from the fox.

Yun got in position to fight the fox.

一路上都是花公鸡在帮助唐云，这次他决心要帮助花公鸡！

唐云做好了和狐狸开战的准备。

Seeing Yun's bravery, the rooster realized it didn't need to be scared anymore. The rooster bit the fox's tail. The pain caused the fox to immediately ran away.

看到唐云那么勇敢，花公鸡不再害怕。它叨住了狐狸的尾巴，狐狸疼得受不了，立刻逃跑了。

Yun finally arrived in the Capital City. He took the exam and was ranked No. 3 on the roll. The Emperor sent him to be an official in a local county.

唐云终于来到京城，参加了考试，名列第三，被皇帝派到一个县城担任县官。

Yun was wise and capable. He successfully governed the people in the county.

Despite this, he would miss his mother every night, who lived thousands of miles away. One day, he was surprised to find that the magical rooster on his outfit was gone.

唐云聪明又能干，把县城治理得井井有条。

尽管如此，一到晚上，他就会思念远方的母亲。一天，他惊讶地发现他衣服上的花公鸡不见了。

"Where did the rooster go?" Yun wondered. Suddenly, he heard "cock-a-doodle-doo" from his court yard.

"花公鸡去哪里了？"唐云很疑惑。这时院子里突然传来"喔喔喔"的叫声。

Yun ran to the court yard. There he saw his mother riding on the back of the rooster.

唐云跑到院子里，看到花公鸡背上坐着一个人，正是自己的母亲！

Yun and his mother were thrilled to reunited with each other.

From then on, Yun's mother lived with him. She continued to embroider fine-quality flowers and animals that looked very life-like.

唐云和母亲高兴地团聚在一起。

从此，母亲一边陪伴唐云一边刺绣。她绣的花草动物还是那样栩栩如生，那样精美。

The Dashing Rooster

The tenth sign of the Chinese zodiac represents dignity with head high. People born in the year of the Rooster pursue perfection filled with fantasy and aspiration. However, the Rooster has to avoid quarrelling with people in order to prove he is right.

神采奕奕的鸡

鸡在十二生肖中排第十，总是昂首挺胸，端庄尊贵。鸡年生人常常大胆幻想，充满抱负，追求尽善尽美。但要注意，不能老是为了说自己是对的，而跟人吵架。

Lunar Years of the Rooster in the Western Calendar

4 February 1921 to 3 February 1922
4 February 1933 to 3 February 1934
4 February 1945 to 3 February 1946
4 February 1957 to 3 February 1958
4 February 1969 to 3 February 1970
4 February 1981 to 3 February 1982
4 February 1993 to 3 February 1994
4 February 2005 to 3 February 2006
3 February 2017 to 3 February 2018
3 February 2029 to 3 February 2030
3 February 2041 to 3 February 2042
3 February 2053 to 3 February 2054

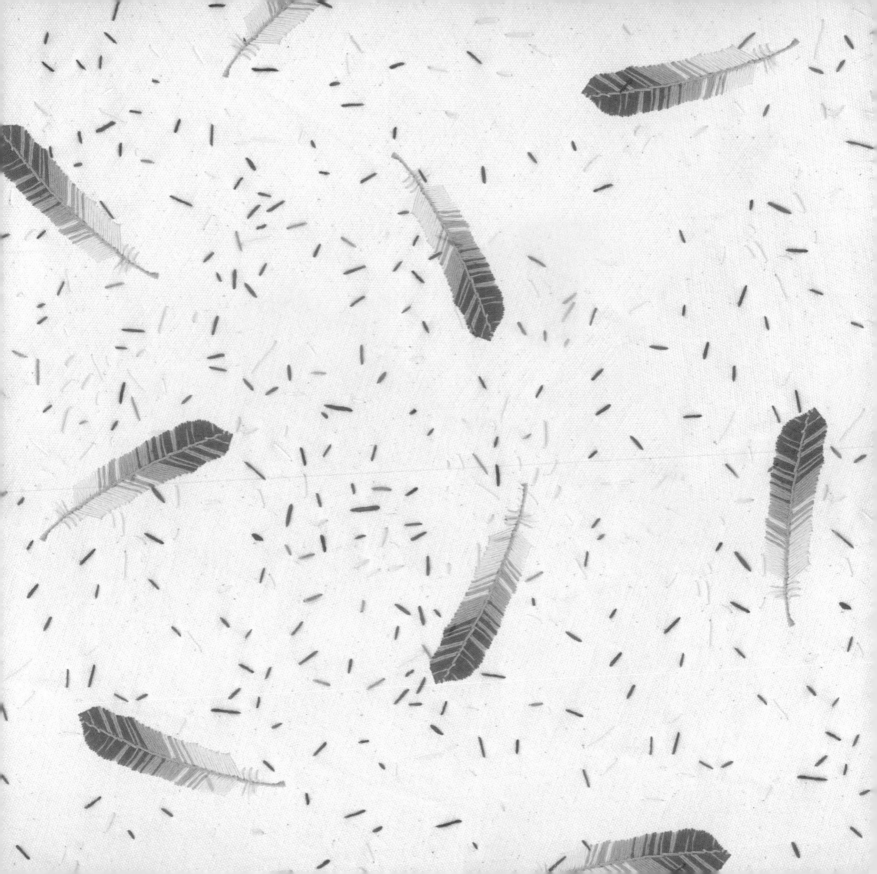

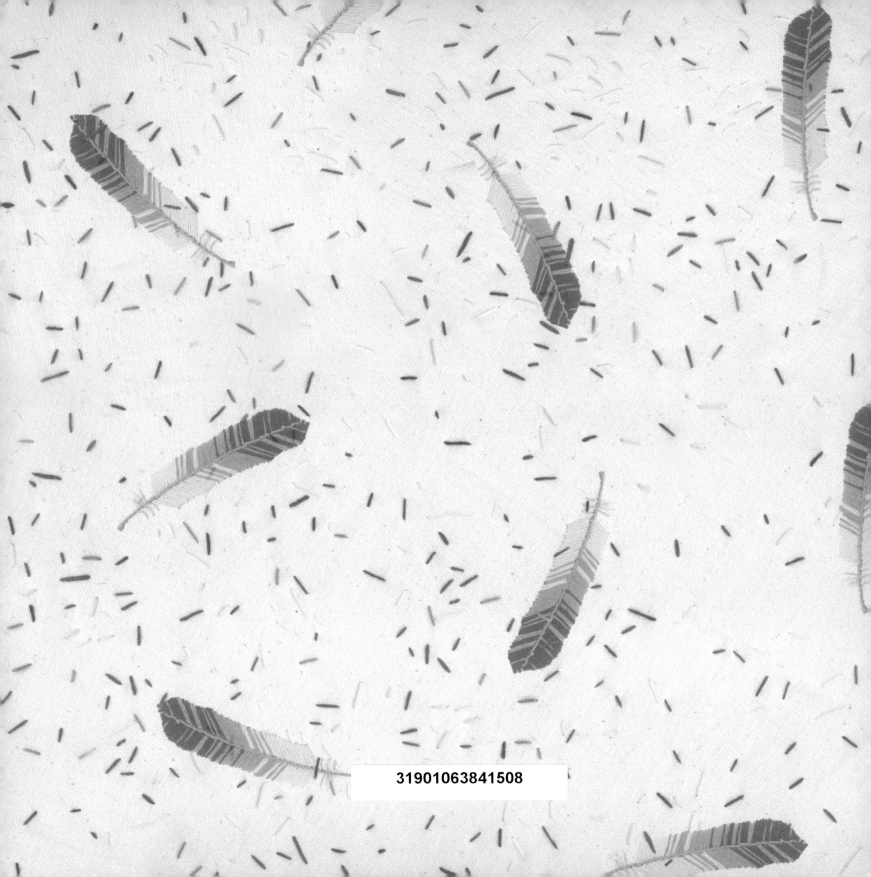